Welcome to London

*To The Gunje family
Thank you so much for attending
and supporting*

By
Elliot Msindo

Dedication

This first novel is dedicated to my dear readers who reminded me that I had not published anything since 2020. It means you have enjoyed my previous work and I will always appreciate your support.

Introduction

Relocating to a new place in the same country can be very stressful. People consider changing jobs, children changing schools, forming new friendships and even learning new language(s). Imagine the stress of migrating outside the country! Imagine migrating to countries outside the continent! People who have migrated to foreign countries in search of greener pastures will definitely resonate with this exhilarating short narrative. Critical issues like weather, culture and environment have been at the forefront of discussions on social media platforms and within communities due to the increase in migration. There are both positive and negative factors raised in the narrative that will trigger critical thinking.

The global society is now very diverse but interconnected due to migration. Tee walks through the journey of migrating to The UK which brings to the forefront topics like intermarriage, religion, racism, culture, sexual abuse, sexuality and family. The story takes place in two parallel settings, Zimbabwe and the UK to give the reader a taste of culturally diverse backgrounds which makes the story more interesting. Tee's life is a representation of millions other migrants who face similar challenges as they try to settle in foreign lands where everyone pursues a better life and better future. The novel follows an exciting fictional

Welcome to London

narrative to identify critical issues affecting people living in the diaspora.

Table of Contents

CHAPTER 1 6
CHAPTER 2 13
CHAPTER 3 20
CHAPTER 4 27
CHAPTER 5 39
CHAPTER 6 51
CHAPTER 7 58
CHAPTER 8 67

CHAPTER 1

The loud and booming music was all she could hear as she watched the lights surrounding her. The disco lights blinded her eyes and the loud music deafened her ears. The pub was filled to the brim mostly with people her age. Tee could only find a tiny space for one of her feet and she regretted going in. It appeared as though a million people had been squashed into a tiny room and packed like tinned sardines but what choice did she have? It was rainy and cold outside inside, it was packed and noisy! Tee found herself stuck to this stranger whose name she could not even remember. With nowhere to go and no money to spend, she had to do what she had to do. Her stomach was rumbling like thunder because of hunger and she felt like she had not eaten in years but this was not a time for that. She had bigger things to worry about. What will she eat? Where will she sleep? These questions played in her mind like a tambourine and they were louder than the booming sound in the Pub. How did she even get here? Tee started retracing her steps.

She remembered dragging her bag towards the bus stop with no clear plan in mind. Events unfolded at a lightning pace and she was still covered in a dark blanket of confusion. She had boarded buses at the bus stop in sight several times, so locating it was not a challenge. However, she had never been out at such a time of the night. What if she is robbed – or rapped – or killed? Tee had grown up to such stories because such things happen in 'ghettos' where she was raised. Her parents had always emphasised the importance of being home before dark and breaching the rule had serious consequences. The streets were always dark and scary at night because of unmaintained street lights which had stopped working ages ago. The few functioning once were normally in low density suburbs or in town. People grew maize in any open spaces creating hood hiding places for robbers and murderers at night. With unemployment skyrocketing because of economic challenges, people resorted to unorthodox ways of acquiring basic needs including robbery. The past few years saw a rise in gun crimes with no clear understanding of where the guns were acquired from. Reports alleged that some guns would be smuggled from South Africa and some out of military camps. Whichever way Tee looked at it, lives of those who moved around at night remained at risk.

Tee's mind was put to rest because in that part of the world, the streets were well lit. The bus stop had a shade which provided some sort of cover from the terrible weather. There was no one at the bus stop and she felt like a lone hunter. Tee could not hear any footsteps or sound except that of the few cars passing intermittently. The cold breeze pierced through her skin and she felt numb. This was made worse by her soggy wet clothes. She reached for her bag and fumbled through a few dry ones. She put on a top and cardigan which left her feeling a bit warm.

Welcome to London

Tee reached for the bus time table which was pasted to the wall of the shade. She had missed the last bus. But where did she actually want to go? Where exactly in town? As her mind was grinding on these questions, a car pulled up and Tee almost jumped.

"Sorry for the ambush! You ok?" A white young man said as he rolled down his window

"I think you missed the last bus." He said before Tee replied

Part of the reason why Tee took time to respond was her lack of confidence in communicating in English. She was still trying to grasp the accent but with very little exposure since she arrived. It was still a mountain climbing task.

"Oh yes I just looked at the timetable." Tee said with a small and soft voice. She was visibly scared and shaken.

"Well, jump in if you are going to town. Are you?" The stranger continued.

Tee was not sure whether to accept the offer or not. There was no time to think about the offer because he was waiting. What if she is kidnapped? Tee wondered. She was caught in between a rock and a hard surface. If she does not accept the lift, how will she get to town? She continued to wonder. What does she intend to do in town anyway? Tee decided to accept the offer. She quietly grabbed her bag and shoved it into the boot.

The good Samaritan drove into town and made a detour as soon as we got to a pub. Nature had called. As always the restroom was filthy and the dark corridors did not make it any better. As soon as he was done he walked towards his new friend.

Welcome to London

Tee's thoughts were disrupted by the stranger who returned with two drinks in his hands and said,

"Here! I bought you prosecco!" The stranger said on top of his voice.

"What is prosecco?" Tee shouted back as loud as she could in her foreign accent. She had never heard such a drink. She wasn't sure whether it was a beverage or water.

"You don't know prosecco?" The stranger looked stunned and wondered which part of the planet Tee came from.

"It's what ladies normally take! Pardon my manners! I should have asked what you drink!" He said with a giggle as he leaned towards Tee's face.

"What's your name?" Tee gathered the courage to ask him.

"Tim!" as he took a sip from his glass seething with beer. "Tim Bots", He said trying to qualify his response.

Tee's eyes shifted towards the stage where there was a band of four rock musicians who were smashing the strings of their guitars. A pool of white faces mobbed them as their fingers danced on the strings. The stage was lit in different colours. The set up was very nice and the lights gave the stage a sparkling appearance. There were no seats so people were either hanging onto each other or holding on to the rails. What surprised her was the amount of people singing along to the songs. The type of music playing was torturous to her because it sounded horrible. Tee had always been under the impression that white people only listen to soft music. She scanned through the crowd and all she could see were a few black faces immersed in the music of the night. They seemed to be

Welcome to London

enjoying themselves while Tee was going through some deep thinking.

Tim held her hand and guided her through a thicket of young people drinking and having a time of their life. It was not easy to identify anyone in there because of congestion so he had to hold her hand tight. Tee felt very uncomfortable being in this absolutely packed place and her head started throbbing. The noise was unbearable and the air was stuffy. All she could think of was how she now hated her aunt who had driven her out of the house and dumped her in this lions' den. Tee had not yet updated her dad about the altercation. She wanted to figure it all out first before detailing her version of events to him. Tim guided Tee to the back where there were relatively fewer people who were smoking. Tim pulled out a cigarette from his back pocket as he showed Tee an empty chair to sit.

"Here! Have one." Tim said as he offered Tee a pack of cigarettes. He did not only smoke but continued to drink like a fish.

"No! No! No! I don't smoke." Tee shrugged her shoulders as she pushed Tim's hand away. Tim was getting confused because Tee was not down for anything. He sat down and started smoking quietly as the night faded away. Tim and Tee had nothing in common but they started chatting about this and that. Tee had her eyes all over the place but she started adjusting to the situation. The night club was a hive of activity. There were a few guys who sat in the corner sniffing some white stuff. In the other corner, she observed two ladies kissing as they smoked the night away. There were four or five girls arguing about snatching each other's men in the middle of the open space. They could hardly stand because alcohol was starting to get the better of

Welcome to London

them. What was funny was that they wanted to throw punches at each other. They were unsure of what they wanted to do but they didn't care. Tee was also unsure whether they were angry or just drunk. What her eyes were witnessing left her bewildered. Tee did not have the courage to ask Tim what was happening because he had gone to top up his beer.

"Are you sure you don't want a drink?" Tim asked as he staggered towards Tee. She last had something to eat about 24 hours ago and with the way things were going, she would not have access to a proper meal in the foreseeable future. She finally gave in and said,

"Do they have coke?" That didn't come out right at all. Tim looked stunned and shocked at the same time. "I don't do coke, sorry!" He said with a straight face which confused Tee the more.

"You neither drink nor smoke but you do coke? Maybe those guys in the corner"

He said as he gestured with his thumb so that they did not see him pointing at them.

"But what they are drinking doesn't look like coke. That's beer" Tee explained because Tim's reaction had shocked her.

"Oh! You mean Coca-Cola?" Tim burst into a very loud laugh which boomed through the ceiling and overrode the loud music.

"I can definitely get you that. If you call it coke, that means something totally different in here." This was news to Tee. She wondered what difference it made. Anyway, her flow

Welcome to London

of thoughts were disrupted by Tim who quickly returned with a glass of Coca-Cola.

Music continued to ramble as the night aged. She was perplexed to notice that it was already in the early hours of the morning. The night had gone so fast and another day was waiting. Tim prompted Tee to finish her drink because the night club was about to close. This triggered a new worry for Tee to know that the pub closes before daybreak. Where will she sleep? She wondered. Her mind was taken back to Harare where she used to see a lot of people in street corners at night. Most of them did not have anywhere to go to and she saw herself being in the same predicament. Tee realised how she had been ungrateful of what she thought were little things like having her own room. Never in a million years had she thought that she would be worried about not having a roof over her head. She realised that she had to either sink or swim. All of a sudden, she felt some dizziness accompanied by a splitting headache after the last swallow. Good sleep normally comes when things are well. The tiredness she felt was unusual for someone with tonnes of things to worry about. Tee felt overwhelmed by heavy sleep and laid her head on the table for a little rest. Tim was keeping an eye on her which gave Tee some assurance. She tried to lift her head but she could only partially do that. Tee's eyes were very heavy and she started having a blurry vision.

"Let's get you home." Were the last words she heard from Tim.

What happened next, remains a guess.

CHAPTER 2

Tee's excitement was engulfed by a cloud of sadness. How do people do it? Leaving everything and everyone behind for years without returning. Tee as she was affectionately known, was busy packing her belongings as she prepared to depart for the so called 'greener pastures'. Life had been pretty comfortable for her until she completed her first degree in Psychology at the University of Zimbabwe. Seconds turned into minutes and minutes into hours as she packed and unpacked her bag. No-one was around so she was talking to herself trying to imagine how life would be like in a new country. It was like leaving an old rag and putting on a new one. Tee was confused about the whole idea of leaving for the diaspora because she did not really understand the reasons why her parents desired for her to go. She didn't care anyway.

Many people had aspirations of living in the diaspora, let alone in London. It is described as the 'Canaan' of this world. Stories in Zimbabwe from those who visited before described how people live a luxurious life. Anyone would afford to drive a car at anytime because they are said to be very cheap. People talk about how they earn thousands per month and even electricity, water and gas are always

Welcome to London

available throughout the year. It is said that jobs are readily available and there is no suffering. Women were overly excited and so was Tee because the cold weather has always been said to give birth to baby-like skin and smoothness. Many ladies would die to have such good skin and Tee was going to be immersed in the cold weather and come out sparkling like an angel.

She imagined herself returning with an entourage after a couple of years. She started having big dreams including building a massive orphanage which she intended to fund single-handedly. The imagination of buying land in one of the posh suburbs of the capital city could not elude her mind as she shoved a slice of bread into her mouth. In her mind, she was telling herself that, 'This is the last time I'm eating this. I will always have pizza and burgers whenever I feel hungry.' Tee started thinking about how she would manage speaking fluent English throughout all conversations. "So, am I going to be speaking in English all the time? What if I cannot understand what they say? What if they laugh at my accent? What if I speak broken English?" These questions lingered in Tee's mind as she suddenly became very nervous. She had not really given careful thoughts to this. How would she manage?

Tee became tired and decided to take a break. She sat at the arm of the chair in her room. There was a lovely photograph of her aunt hanging on the wall. This was the same aunt who would pick her up at the Airport when she reached London. Tee didn't care about where in London. All she knew was that they would meet at the airport. Her aunt was someone she had never really managed to have a conversation with about life in London. "When I text you on WhatsApp, you take ages to respond. Even a day or two.

Welcome to London

How will I know about London if I can't talk to you?" Tee was talking to herself as she took a breather. Her aunt was always a busy woman. "She must be a busy woman." Tee thought to herself as she tried to understand her aunt's 'weird schedule.' "She must have a very important job but anyway, we will see when we get there." Tee was wondering why her aunt had not yet managed to buy some piece of land in the posh areas to build a mansion. She just owned a 'normal house' in the medium density residential area of the capital city. "You have been in London for 20 years but you have not yet managed to build a mansion. Why? That will never happen when I start working. In 3 years, I will be a landlady." The thoughts about her aunt's lack of investment back home boggled her. She was convinced that her aunt must own a mansion in London which is why she was not interested in building one back home. Tee was quite disappointed though that her aunt did not live in London.

It's a common assumption in Zimbabwe that everyone who is based in England lives in London. So, when she was bidding her friends farewell, she just said 'I'm leaving for England.' And their immediate reply was, "Wow! Lucky you. Please, Tee remember us when you get to London. We have always been your friends through thick and thin" referring to many incidents she sneaked out of the house to meet her boyfriend.

There was one particular occasion when her dad and mum had left for town and she decided to do the unthinkable. Trevor, her boyfriend did not live very far. Her pulse still increases whenever she thought of this incident even to this day. After gathering courage, she invited Trevor to her house and he took no time to arrive. They started being

Welcome to London

naughty in the lounge since she thought they had the whole house to themselves. When they had shut the world outside, in the hype of the moment, blood boiling and kisses raining, the door was suddenly knocked. In panic and confusion, she jumped from the sofa where they were cuddling and headed straight for the kitchen door so that she could jump out of the window. She never thought how she was going to explain Trevor's presence in the lounge. As soon as she was about to open the window, Shylet, her best friend started calling from outside. She was the one who was knocking. Tee vividly remembers the incident and the memory of it made her knees melt like jelly. The story does not end there! As soon as she let Shylet in, her parents walked in behind her and there they were: Trevor, Shylet and Tee.

Questions and answers raced through Tee's mind and there was hardly any time to come up with a lie. Her dad was a 'no nonsense guy' so Tee knew that her world had finally crumbled. She sank into the sofa behind her because her body was overwhelmed by the tension in the room. That was when Shylet leapt in to save the day. Tee's dad had met Shylet many times so seeing her at their place was not a surprise. He looked at Tee expecting her to start saying something but she was tongue tied. Tee felt as if her dad was reading a book containing all the naughtiness they had been up to since they left. She did not have time to look at what was happening to Trevor. She just imagined that maybe he had already wet his pants because of fear because Tee's dad is a well-built and gigantic man. His eyes pierced through Tee's heart and she could not remain on her feet anymore. This moment seemed to have lasted a lifetime but Tee doubted if it was even more than a couple of minutes.

Welcome to London

"Hi daddy. How has your day been? We are on our way from the shops so we decided to pass by checking up on Tee. This is my cousin, Trevor. He recently moved here to live with us after completing his 'A' Levels."

Since that day, Tee had always been indebted to Shylet. She bailed her out of a precarious situation which was going to spell an end to her dreams, freedom and potentially, her life. Tee does not remember how they left the house but her father was left perturbed at her reaction because she just froze and sank into the nearest sofa. Anyway, he did not say anything and Shylet always reminds Tee of this incident. It had always become her punchline when she wanted something.

"Friend, remember I am always your right-hand woman even when you are in London! Don't find anyone to replace me" Shylet said jokingly. "I should be the first one to receive the pounds before your parents even do" she continued. "I know chommie. I will send you a truckload of pounds so that you never have to go to work ever again." Tee said as she gave in to Shylet's demands.

Tee was still fixated on the photo as these memories played out in her mind. She started to think about her friends and felt very sad. "Maybe I will apply for a Visa for them to join me after a few months since I will be earning a significant amount." She comforted herself with those words. She remembered the nasty fight she had with Trevor because he did not want her to relocate to London. He said he would not see her off because he was opposed to the relocation. He reminded her of the promises they made of being there for each other through thick and thin. Tee and Trevor had a rendezvous where they used to meet almost every day. Tee remembered Taku, a boy from their

Welcome to London

hood who ended up spray painting their names on the small bridge where they used to meet. Trevor was furious with Tee and he viewed this just as good as a break-up. Tee was torn in two. The desire of living a luxurious life in a first-world country where life was smooth, flowing like still waters and listening to Trevor. All the talk of having three children, owning a car, and personalising the number plates to the initials of their children seemed to be slipping through her fingers. Wearing shirts that look alike as they went shopping in town and building a massive house in the affluent suburbs of the capital city sounded like just a fallacy at this moment. These fantasies seemed to have been flashed down the drain. Trevor was the love of her life but she couldn't let this opportunity slip away. Tee had told herself that she would never love anyone else and she would make things right with Trevor when he calmed down. As soon as she got to London, Tee promised herself to rebuild the broken walls of their relationship by applying for a visa for him to join her. That would be their 'happily ever after.' But wait a minute, there was one more thing to worry about.

"How does flying feel like? Are there bumps in the sky? Does the plane fly above or below the clouds? Can I be able to see the pilot? So, what do I do when I feel hot?" Excitement and fear overtook her as the questions raced through her mind. She tried to imagine the experience from start to finish.

"So how does that huge thing suspend in the air? How many people will be in the plane? So will the clouds be below or above the plane?" These questions boggled her and she started thinking about how it would feel like being high up. Tee struggled to know whether to be afraid or

Welcome to London

excited because this was going to be her first experience. The luxury of adjusting the seat and sleeping mid-air could not elude Tee's mind. She just had a vague idea from watching movies and stories from others but her time was almost near. Tee hardly had any sleep because she could not wait for her departure date. She had no Trevor nor Shylet in her mind. She just had the flying experience occupying her mind.

CHAPTER 3

Heathrow Airport as she later knew it to be, was a busy hive. People were walking hurriedly in every direction. Apparently, everyone seemed to know where they were going except Tee. She could not understand how so many people could be at a single place at the same time. She could hardly see any unoccupied space as people shuffled on. Thousands of people flocked in one direction and others, in the opposite direction. Tee held tight to her wallet which had a few dollars remaining because such congested areas are favourite hunting grounds for pick pocketers. Little did she know that she was in a different world altogether. She never thought about the language barrier but as soon as she saw all the people from different nationalities, she wondered how they all communicated.

"Join the queue! Everyone who is from the EU to the left! All British passport holders join the middle queue! Everyone else, to the right!"

An immigration officer barked and people shuffled to the right and to the left. As a black person, she was used to being 'everyone else' so Tee did not find that offensive. People were packed like newspapers in an old van as they queued for the British precious stamp. Everyone seemed

Welcome to London

to know what they were doing except Tee. As the queue moved along, Tee's heart started pounding like a tread mill.

"What if I don't make it through the security?"

The thought of being deported haunted her because she had heard stories of people who were not allowed to pass through immigration offices for one reason or the other. She remembers the misfortune her distant cousin who tried to embark on this journey to greener pastures had met when she was denied the precious stamp. Tee couldn't bear the thought of dragging her two big bags back home. The excitement engulfs a lot of people and the word of going to London spreads faster than veld fire in ghetto suburbs. Her cousin stayed in her room for more than a month after the deportation because the embarrassment was unbearable. Her family was very bitter because after her deportation, they had consulted a 'so called prophet' who said that there was a family member who had cast a spell on her. Ever since that time, relations within Tee's extended family fell apart. She was always baffled by the fact that there are numerous churches in Zimbabwe yet many people still lived in poverty. There are the white garment churches and the fancy ones for nicely dressed 'men of God' who are now jokingly called 'men of Gold' in the streets because of their love for money. They amass as much wealth as they can while doing anything possible to be popular.

"Never tell anyone until you have made it through! Handidi zvekuzonyara ini!" Tee's mum had said as she shoved the last clothes into her bag.

Tee's mum had done all the packing and the parcels were well labelled. They were all aware that they could not

Welcome to London

exceed 46 kilograms so after adding every bit, Tee's dad was called in to weigh the bags.

"Haa zvadarikidza izvi!" Tee's mum vent her frustration as she was fed up because of packing and unpacking the bags.

"I think we will leave them like that. Unongokumbirawo kuti please, just this one time," She said standing akimbo.

She wiped her sweaty face with the back of her left hand while scanning the 2 bags lying in front of her. She had started working on the bags for the past week or so. The obsession of packing was driven by the pain of losing her daughter and apparently not seeing her for years. The anxiety of not knowing how things could go killed her but she had to accept the situation. There were a lot of people who went abroad and stayed there for years. Some have struggled to visit because of not having necessary documents to travel so if they leave the UK to Zimbabwe, they would never return.

"Ah mama, Ndinokumbira ani? Asi munoti ibhazi reBulawayo here? There is no conductor to negotiate with." Tee said jokingly as they both giggled while trying to figure out what to do next.

The bags were packed with nzungu, Cerevita, Nyimo, chimukuyu and dovi. It is very common amongst Africans to carry traditional food to the UK because they are rare commodities and they are quite expensive. Tee had been raised in a middle income family so she could afford good food. She usually went out for a meal at Nandos in an area called Avenues in Harare once a month for some nice food with her parents. She also carried fond memories of her boyfriend taking her to Sam levy village in Borrowdale

Welcome to London

where there is a Chicken inn restaurant, fancy shops and some fresh air. She was not the type of a girl who was into these traditional foods. When they were growing up, eating things like Nyimo, chimukuyu and dovi was regarded as being rural-minded so in order to maintain her social status, she had always avoided such foods. Most girls did likewise.

Tee's drifting mind was driven back from wander land by the officer controlling the queue who said, "Next! Point number 4 please!" as he pointed to his right. Such an order does not work very well with, 'Please' where Tee comes from but it was not the right time to think about that.

The queue was moving faster than a jumbo jet and as she made her way to the counter, she started sweating. The fear of uniformed people has always been a thing for her because in Zimbabwe, the Police and Armed forces are rarely friendly to a civilian unless they are receiving a bribe or humiliating them. She vividly remembered what happened on her way to R.G Mugabe Airport when they were stopped at a roadblock along Airport road.

"Licence, registration, and triangle" A stern-faced officer ordered without a greeting. His uniform was shabby and his boots were worn out on the left side. He had dry lips which he continuously licked and red eyes that pierced through the thick blanket of darkness covering the other side of the road. "Where are you going and why?" The officer asked.

"To the Airport to drop off my daughter." Tee's dad replied. "You have to park your car because the tail light is not working." Tee's dad looked confused and bewildered because the car had been working just fine before they left home. He just followed the instructions although they

Welcome to London

risked running late. Tee was getting increasingly agitated. The tail light was actually working when her dad checked and asked the Police officer if they can leave but he wouldn't let them off the hook that easily.

"So now you think I am stupid? The fact that it is now working proves that it is faulty because it wasn't!" The officer raised his voice and two other officers joined in.

"Mdhara ari kuda kuoma musoro uyu. The old man is trying to be hot-headed!" "Manje munoparara pano mukaita zvedzungu!" He continued teasing Tee's dad.

After what seemed like eternity, the other officer walked to Tee's dad and said, "Mdhara kana muchida kubaya motombotionawo." As each minute passed, Tee's frustration grew because she was running out of time. There were three other police officers with rifles in their hands circling the car like hungry hyenas. What happened after that, is a story for another day.

Tee started to examine herself to make sure that nothing was amiss. The immigration officer looked intently at her and nodded. That short moment felt like it had taken ages because of fear. The officer's sharp look stopped her breath and she wanted to run away. When she went through the barriers, she laughed at herself because such unbearable fear almost led to wetting her pants. Moving out of one's comfort zone is never easy. Tee felt very small and tiny in a sea full of big fish. She felt so inferior. Not knowing what to do next, made the experience even harder.

Tee was swarmed by a pool of white faces and she felt embarrassed to be black. She had never seen so many white people in her life. Ever since the "Hondo yeminda" debacle, most white people deserted Zimbabwe to

Welcome to London

neighbouring countries like South Africa and Zambia. The few who remained, went underground so it was very rare to run into a white person except for those who did their shopping at posh places like Sam Levy Village where white people have mansions tucked in extremely quiet areas. An average black family cannot afford properties in such areas and those who do, are from rich backgrounds. Their children attend highly esteemed schools like Peterhouse, Falcon College, and St George's college. The latter is located right next to The State House. They also have the luxury of studying abroad but Tee's parents did not have such kind of wealth. She looked around and her presence seemed to be tainting the whiteness around her. How possible is it to feel so much pressure before anyone says anything? She wondered as she manoeuvred through a group of people waiting for their friends and relatives. Tee had never felt so small, so minute and so useless until that moment. She could not locate her aunt among the many people. She dragged her bags from left to right but she could not see her. Fear gripped her because of the feeling of abandonment. The waiting period turned into a nightmarish experience.

"Is this London?" Tee sighed as she looked at people walking in and out of the Airport. What surprised her was the confidence shown by most people walking in who seemed to know where they were heading to. Time was running out and she did not have a phone. Tee thought of asking for a phone from a stranger but she did not have the courage to do so because her confidence had just sipped away like water into a crevice.

Welcome to London

'How can a black girl ask for a phone from a white man? What kind of words does she use? What if I don't understand the accent?'

All these questions populated Tee's mind and she just couldn't. The weather was horrible and she started shivering. She recalled her mum's words,

"Remember to wear warm clothes. Your aunt always says that the weather is very unfriendly."

Tee didn't care because her mind was thinking about the 'London experience' so the heavy coat was left hanging behind the door in her room as she rushed for the car. After one long hour, she saw her aunt walking through and she gave a deep sigh of relief…

CHAPTER 4

"This is how it is amainini. Welcome to the UK. There is no time to play! You are now an adult so you have to work. They are expecting you to send money back home to look after them. You also have to pay for the room you are using. Electricity, gas, and water bill we split in half. I cannot afford to take care of an adult while you just eat, sleep and fart." Tee's aunt shouted. Tears started rolling down Tee's cheeks as she felt the pain of not being in the comfort of her parents' home nor her boyfriend.

"I tried aunt but the job was difficult." She said, "The place was smelly and I couldn't stand it." She continued as she wiped off her tears.

"It was full of old people and I had to lift them and clean them. that's too much. I can't manage…" Tee continued as she sobbed.

Zimbabwe is a country built on very strong kinship ties and so is Africa. Extended family is very important and valued. Tee's dad came from a big family. He has five brothers and three sisters. Tee remembered visiting them numerous times as she was growing up. She had cousins who also visited them during school holidays. They used to gather during popular holidays like Christmas and New year. It was

Welcome to London

the best time of Tee's life because her grandparents used to slaughter a beast each time there was a family reunion. Tee had met almost every member of her extended family except her UK-based aunt. She also knew that her aunt had a daughter who was in her twenties but she had never met her. Once in a while, Tee's aunt forced her daughter to speak to Tee and her family over the phone. They all never understood why she always spoke in English. It was surprising to learn that her aunt's daughter he did not know Shona. She actually never wanted anything to do with the language. She had grown up in London and she did not see herself going to Zimbabwe where 'there are mosquitos and flies all over' according to her words. Her accent was difficult to understand and she spoke so fast. Oftentimes, Tee would hear her yelling at her mum and telling her that she does not want to talk to strangers.

Each of Tee's uncles had a house built at the rural compound in Shurugwi. The compound was big and nicely maintained. Tee enjoyed the drive because of the beautiful scenery along the way. They normally started their journey early in the morning because it was a good five hour drive. Their first stop was in Kwekwe at Truckers' Inn where her dad would spoil them with buns and Coca-Cola. Tee also remembered a handful of women whose market stalls were patched in front of the Supermarket. They normally sold boiled nuts, boiled mealie cobs, a bunch of bananas and bottled water. To the left, were shabbily dressed men roasting green cobs. Each time a bus, a truck or bus pulled up, they would sprint with a handful of roasted cobs tightly gripped in their hands trying to make a sell. Tee's family spent about half an hour before taking off and Tee watched as these men sprinted more than five times under her watch.

Welcome to London

They passed through Gweru and into Shurugwi town. Tee did not like sleeping along the way because she was scared of the famous Boterekwa. That part of the road had claimed many lives because the road is badly damaged. It also meanders like a river and inexperienced drivers found it difficult to manoeuvre. What has always fascinated Tee is how the mountain was sliced like a piece of bread to construct a road which passes through it. She glanced to the left with fear as the car slowly descended and her anxiety went through the roof. Each time she passed through Boterekwa, it felt like a new experience but she could not recall how many times she had passed through it. There is a steep slope to the left where one can only view tree tops. Far ahead, a carpet of green canopies can only be viewed and stories of cars rolling down the slope have always been around for donkey years. To the right, the half sliced mountain stands tall with protruding tree roots smiling at each passing car. During rainy season, there were frequent occurrences of mudslide and giant trees falling into the road.

They used to pass through Chachacha on their way home but since the full function of Unki Mine, they use the newly constructed tarred road which leads to the Mine. When the Mine became fully operational years ago, local communities were very optimistic that some noticeable development would be witnessed but there has been nothing of note for Tee except that tarred road which ends at the Mine. Tee had heard that there was a little donation to a local secondary school but that's just it. People still tread the dusty roads and they still struggle to access clean water. Enough about Unki Mine – Tee enjoyed the sight of the smooth-flowing Mutevekwi river. There were a few guys with their legs dipped into the river panning gold.

Welcome to London

They normally lifted their heads to shout a few obscenities before bending down to continue with their treasure hunt.

Tee enjoyed the sight of his grandpa who always waited by the gate and directed her dad through the gate with a beaming smile. He waited by the doorside and hugged her so tight and said,

"Masvika ka vahosi!" loosely translated to say, 'You have arrived, senior wife.'

He always called Tee his wife and the rest of Tee's cousins. Her granny would be performing little dances in front of the car while ululating as loud as she could. She tried to teach Tee how to ululate but she never mastered the art. Her bare feet raised some dust which went through the car window but she did not care. Tee and her family were normally the last ones to arrive. Tee and her cousins did not waste any precious time, they quickly got together to play until the cows came home. They were as many as fourteen. They played well into the night until their grandma called them to eat.

They were usually enough plates for adults but all the kids had to share and dig in from a few plates placed in front of them. Grandma only separated boys from girls and would give equal shares of meat to avoid scrambles for the precious pieces. Tee and her cousins all dug in with half of their palms still covered in dust. They did not care because they were determined to go back to their self-made playing field. All the adults sat around a big fire sharing different life stories from around Zimbabwe and South Africa. The aunties sat in the main kitchen with their sister-in laws and grandma enjoyed running around with Tee and the other kids outside. The clear blue sky splattered by bright stars at night provided good environment to play.

Welcome to London

The clear moon hung over their homestead and smiled at the children who were having a time of their life.

Families have always shared such bonds and when parents grow old, adult children take turns to look after them. It is usually the responsibility of daughters to look after their parents when they are no longer able to look after themselves. Extended families take turns to support them. There are not many Care homes in Zimbabwe as it is considered gross neglect to send parents into a care home because it is not part of the African culture. Young boys and girls are not normally given the responsibility to look after the sick or the elderly so it was a cultural shock for Tee who was electrocuted by the experience. Not only were they old but they were more than forty elderly people with varying ailments. She was shocked to see several men running around and providing personal care to some elderly women. They undressed them, gave them a shower and helped them to dress. Tee had not been mentally prepared for such a cultural shift so she quietly grabbed her small handbag and sneaked out of the premises using the back door.

Tee was shaken out of the deep memories by her aunt who continued the rant and said, "Shut up!" her aunt said, interjecting her thoughts.

"Is the money you get going to be smelly? Will it carry any sign showing that you got it from old people? Will the shops reject it because it is from old people? You have to grow up and be responsible!" She said wagging her pointing finger in Tee's face.

"This is your new life. You have siblings and you need to look after them. Give your parents a break. If you want to be a slay queen then leave my house and find somewhere

Welcome to London

else to go. We can't flash five thousand pounds down the drain."

She said this in a loud voice banging the table with her fist. If the table had a voice, it could have cried out with pain. Thank God it did not break in half.

"Which five thousand?" Tee hesitantly asked

"Do you think coming here was a donation from a charity? Zvawakatozungaira mwana iwe!" She chided.

This was the first time Tee had heard about the five thousand pounds. She later discovered that some people moving to the UK via some agencies were paying a certain amount to get sponsorship visas. There are middlemen who also charge exorbitant prices to connect desperate people with recruiters. Corruption always finds its way in such circumstances. Stories of people selling their cars and houses to fund moves to the UK have been in circulation because of the desire to go abroad. Bogus recruiters are also now awash on the internet and some have been scammed of their hard-earned money. Opportunists always lie in wait to seize such opportunities. Accommodation is another area that has been taken advantage of. People relocating will definitely need housing and some have been duped by scammers who advertise houses that are either non-existent or not on the market. The moment money is deposited into their bank accounts, they vanish without a trace. It is also believed that some of them do not even live in the UK. Marketplace on Facebook has been a breeding ground for some of these scammers. It is not only difficult but sad that such desperate people are caught unaware. This was what Tee's aunt was talking about. The hefty amount they paid for her to get sponsorship.

Welcome to London

Tee's aunt was pretty annoyed because she had grudgingly contributed a large chunk of the five thousand pounds with the remaining balance coming from Tee's dad. She had also put in the hard work to find a sponsor only for Tee to throw that in her face. Tee went to work and returned home after working just a couple of hours. The same agency that sponsored her to the UK had several other young girls working for it. Tee started to realise that all that glitters is not gold. She started thinking about how happy she was back home with friends coming around to see her. She never experienced this loneliness and isolation in her entire 22 years. After ditching the job, She spent most of her time alone indoors because her aunt was never home. She left for work at around 06:30 and returned late around 8 pm. She would bath and go straight to bed. Tee and her aunt were like strangers renting the same apartment. During her off days, she would pick extra shifts with another care agency so she was hardly home.

Her aunt's daughter had since moved out when she started University. She had only returned once and did not even take time to talk to Tee. She was this slim and tall girl who had a pierced nose. She was so much into rings. She had a nose ring, tongue ring, ear rings and multiple other rings on her fingers. Her nails were artificially long and Tee wondered how she prepared any food. On the day she came, she had long braided hair that looked nice on her. She was aware that Tee had arrived a few weeks back but she was not particularly interested in any conversation with her. She walked in and they exchanged greetings and she vanished into her mother's bedroom. When Tee finished preparing supper, she came out and grabbed her plate. She sat on the sofa but most her time, she was glued to her phone. She flipped from one social media platform

Welcome to London

to another. The whole encounter left Tee feeling as if she was non-existent. After eating, she left her plate on the sofa and went away. She did not help with doing the dishes or cleaning. She did not even bother to thank Tee for the food. She owned a grey mini cooper which looked very nice. Tee was not sure where she disappeared to but she returned in the early hours of the morning.

Her aunt's daughter was not yet married but she was living with a man she called her partner. Tee was a little confused with these terms because such arrangements are simply called cohabiting back home. These sort of arrangements are rarely brought to the attention of parents or respected relatives but her aunt seemed to be very aware of what was happening and she was comfortable with it. They were living together but not married. Tee felt she had a lot to learn about the new culture she was getting into. Life seemed to continue as normal for everyone. All these things went through her mind as she encountered the wrath of her aunt.

"What kind of life is this?" Tee wondered as she tried to understand how people function in this country.

During her free time, Tee would go to town for window shopping. She always hoped to bump into people she could befriend but this never happened. The town had few people walking around, especially in the morning. Later in the day, most people were the elderly doing their weekly shopping and a couple of young white faces. On the bus, Tee normally used to sit with very lovely, elderly white people who would initiate conversations with her but because of not understanding their British accent, she would just smile and nod. Life had never been so miserable for her. She was almost going mad. Can you

Welcome to London

imagine what happens when excitement turns into disappointment? She looked at the houses and flats and compared them to her parents' house. Houses are spacious and beautiful with big yards in Zimbabwe. These ones are just uniform as if they were designed for refugees. The rooms are tiny which can only fit a few items. Tee could not understand how people have adjusted to this kind of life. When people talk about England, everyone starts wishing they could migrate because it is viewed as 'The Garden of Eden.' They don't know how much Tee wished she could run and never come back. With these thoughts, she covered her head with a plastic bag so that her wig was not drenched and darted home. It was raining cats and dogs.

Tee's aunt had not spoken to her since their altercation. She did not even want to eat the food Tee prepared. The relationship between them became frosty before it even started. She knew she was back from work. One of those rare days when she came back early. Tee opened the door and there she was waiting for her to come back. Tee wondered what she had done wrong this time.

"I supported you to come here so that you can have better opportunities!", She said angrily without even giving Tee a chance to put her second foot through the door. Tee scanned through the room in a split second and noticed that her few belongings had been gathered and heaped into a corner. No one ever sat on the couch except for today so Tee sensed that all hell was about to break loose. Her voice thundered through the room and when she stood up, Tee felt like a tiny ant. Tee's aunt was well built just like her dad. Her eyes were sharper than King Tshaka's assegai and her direct confrontation seemed to have lasted a lifetime.

Welcome to London

Tee could not help but just shed tears. She was not sure why she was crying but she knew she had already dropped four or five teardrops. The situation had escalated quicker than she anticipated and with her clothes gathered in the corner, she knew what was coming next.

"Is this how you repay me? Lying around as if you are a princess in paradise? Do you think you came here for your honeymoon?" Tee's aunt went on barking. She was fuming and Tee had an idea why she was angry. The job.

"Bills don't pay themselves! You pay for what you use and since you don't want to listen to me, it means you are an adult so go and find your own place. Take your belongings! Out you go!".

For a moment, Tee thought her aunt was joking. She had been in the UK for barely a month. Tee had not even managed to get her head around things let alone finding her own place.

"This can't be. My aunt cannot do this!" She thought as she tried to pull her other foot through the door but she did not even feel her foot because of the tense atmosphere. The echoes of her aunt's voice still played in her ears. Tee was sure that her aunt was still talking but she was no longer listening to her words. Tee was now absorbed in a pool of thoughts that she had no time to digest the venom from her aunt's mouth. She had not even uttered a word as this appeared to be a one-woman show. Tee tried to open her mouth but her tiny little voice was not enough to override her aunt's booming sound. The more Tee stood there transfixed, the angrier her aunt became.

"But aunt I am sorry! Please aunt forgive me! I don't have anywhere to go! Please don't do this!" Tee finally got a few

Welcome to London

pleas out of her mouth after several attempts. What she said seemed to have infuriated her aunt the more.

"I don't care and I don't want to care! Take your things now and out! out!" The emphasis on 'Out!' showed how determined she was to kick Tee out. No amount of pleas seemed to work because she had already made up her mind. She shoved Tee out of the door with so much force that she almost broke her arm and locked the door from inside. She went berserk and started throwing Tee's clothes out of the window. She squeezed the last item, Tee's monarch through the window and vanished into the corridor. Tee could not believe what had just happened. It was still raining but the drops drowned her tears and she felt numb. Her clothes were smiling in the rain as they soaked as much as they could before they were gathered by their owner. It was night-time. She was all alone with no plan and no money.

Tee saw the dim light in her aunt's room fading away as she struggled to get a grip of what had just happened. She had been standing there for what seemed like hours when she was startled by a cat mewing. She slowly bent down to pick her stuff up one after the other. She was hoping that her aunt would come to check up on her or open the door but midnight was almost approaching yet she was still standing akimbo. She knocked several times but the door was never opened. Tee slowly dragged herself down the concrete stairs tears flowing like the river Nile. She felt so much anger and hatred towards her aunt building inside her. The feeling of being rejected consumed her. She vowed that she was never coming back to this 'woman's' house. Tee had been raised by very lovely parents who never treated her like dirt. Her parents were traditional but

Welcome to London

flexible enough to appreciate the evolving world since they lived in an urban area. Her academic journey was very smooth and even though they were not rich, they showed her love. Her bag bumped into the iron bars but at that moment, she didn't care much. She looked back to bid farewell to what had been her home for a couple of weeks. The streetlights greeted her with amusement and the silence shook her hand as she embarked on a journey to nowhere. She was convinced that it was very cold but the coldness was the least of her worries. Tee was soaked to the marrow. Her shoes were heavy and squelchy but she didn't care. This is life. **WELCOME TO LONDON.**

CHAPTER 5

"Who's this?" Chen said as she picked up a call on her mobile phone that had several missed calls. She could not reach the phone easily because it was buried under aprons, gloves, and boxes stashed on her front passenger's seat. The car was filled up to the brim with bits and bobs. The only available space was the driver's seat. She had empty boxes of chocolate; fast food remains and empty water bottles all scattered at the back seat. There was an unfamiliar smell coming from the car but Chen had been so used to it that it didn't bother her anymore. The car boot was already filled up with spare uniforms and some greasy, out-of-date tinned foods. She normally went straight to a night shift after finishing homecare calls. Blankets occupied half of her back seat because when she did not get a chance to go back home as what often happened, she just covered herself for a quick nap at the back seat. She remembered one occasion when she spent a week without returning home because she had to work extra hard. Sleeping is a luxury at times when there is too much work.

Chen often drove from one client to another and time is of paramount importance in Domiciliary care business. Her

Welcome to London

rota had been hectic, especially the past week because of staff going off sick due to Covid. She had been running her care agency since 2018 when she started it with a friend of hers. The profit margins had plummeted during the Covid outbreak so her company was almost on its knees. She faced serious staff shortage which led to high turnover of carers so she had to do the work herself. Staffing issues are affecting most care agencies all over the UK. NHS is reportedly gripped with the same challenges so she did not have very high hopes of having her care agency operating at full capacity anytime soon.

It came as a shock to most people when The UK's Home Office allowed care agencies to recruit from abroad. When the opportunity arose, Chen grabbed it with both hands as her care agency was already on its knees because of lack of staff. Chen was not sure how she was going to fund for certificates of sponsorship but she knew somehow things would work out. This opportunity soon presented an unforeseen window of making more money by charging a certain amount in exchange for a certificate of sponsorship. Chen was not the only one doing it. Several other recruiters had not hesitated to make it count. Word spread like veld fire as people scrambled for places to complete nurse aid training courses and English proficiency examinations. Red Cross and St. Johns were the most popular trainers and they were inundated by applications from desperate men and women who could not wait to leave for greener pastures. The whole stampede painted a picture of caged lions trying to scramble their way to freedom. No one ever wanted to miss out on this opportunity. The desperation opened a whole new door to modern slavery, sexual exploitation and financial abuse which no one had foreseen although not

Welcome to London

surprising. People were willing to do anything to go abroad but can you blame them? People never dared to ask what kind of a job they would be doing, how they would survive and how much they would get as remuneration. Most people just said 'it is better to get something to live on than to live on nothing'. And so the mass exodus began as people paid thousands of dollars to acquire certificates of sponsorship. Remember, such mass exodus from Zimbabwe is not a new phenomenon because there was one in the early 2000s so this felt like déjà vu for some people.

Chen as she is affectionately known, left Zimbabwe back in 2001 when the economy started to nosedive. How did she even get the name Chen? Well most people migrating to the UK with traditional African names have tried to modify their names to make it easy for the owners of the country. The likes of Mushaningas' have started calling themselves 'Mush', The Tanakas' call themselves 'Tan', The Chengetos' call themselves 'Chen.' The list goes on and on. Her full name was Chengeto. This was just a way of trying to fit into the white community because a lot of the British people found it difficult to pronounce foreign names so in order to make life easy for them, people would just modify their names to suit their work environment. This mainly relates to identity crisis which has affected a lot of families because of trying to alter their identity so that they can fit into the new community. Some people do not care much because at the end of the day, what matters to them is a fat pay cheque.

Chen's situation is not an isolated incident because the ripple effects spread from cultural identity, religious identity, dress code and even food. The colonial mind-set

Welcome to London

is still engrained and engraved in some black people's minds so their views tend to be biased towards everything Western including colour, ideas and education. Inferiority complex is buried within their bloodstream so much that even children who are born, struggle to see their value as long as they're black. Back in the days, it was a spectacle to see a white person in the ghettos.

The superiority of the white race jogs the memory back to when all the young boys of schoolgoing age used to play football in the streets. It was a norm that towards sunset, streets would be turned into mini 'National stadiums' as they were affectionately known. It was a shame to miss the game and young boys played as if their lives depended on the games. The famous players of that time included Zimbabwe's very own Peter Ndlovu, Nigerian, Jay Jay Okocha, Ghanaian, Stephen Appiah and South African, Benny McCarthy. There are very few occasions when these games ended in peace but they never stopped anyway. Most boys all went home with bruised eyes, cut toes or swollen ankles but that was not enough to deter them from blocking the streets the following afternoon to kick the ball.

Mrs Murombo's gate faced one of the popular streets which was turned into a mini stadium. A strict retired headmistress who was as straight as an arrow. She did not tolerate any nonsense and weekend afternoons were the most traumatic for her. The mixture of screaming and crying from both boys and girls were like a gravy made of peaches, monkey apples and tomatoes if that ever exists. Mrs Murombo would bark from inside her fence but her voice quickly drowned in the cheers, boos and screams of children having a time of their life. The dilapidating tarred

Welcome to London

roads had seen better days so to suffice, they should just be called dusty streets of the ghetto. There were patches of tar which stood out as evidence that they were once tarred streets which are now riddled with puddles. Mrs Murombo had previously tried using a long stick to whip one or two boys before but they easily outran her and she was too old to catch up with any of them. Upon reflection, such shenanigans caused her so much grief which led to her grave.

Funny enough, children were still using the street in front of her house as a mini stadium two years ago. It was during one of these August afternoons during school holidays when people caught a glimpse of a white man strolling the dusty streets of the ghetto. The reaction was mutual from all of the boys playing in the streets because they all ran towards him for a closer glimpse or if lucky enough, a feel of his skin. He was mobbed by what appeared like a million people and people wondered how he even survived the stampede, let alone breathe. All the boys hung to the fence of the house he went in, waiting for him to come out so that they could catch another glimpse. The wait went on until the dark hours of the night when some decided to retire to their houses. Funny enough, the congregation waiting for him also included older men and women. The wait was synonymous to the Biblical teachings on the second coming of Jesus always taught in Sabbath school where no one knows when he will come. A few verses ran through people's minds as they waited anxiously with a few others hanging around. Mosquitoes were not able to convince them to abandon ship with their bites. They had bigger things to look forward to. The wait was long and no one knew when the white man was going to come out. Inferiority is still ingrained in many people and it will

Welcome to London

continue to live on until there is a deliberate effort to liberate the mind from oppression. Where does that start? How can that be done? Many have pondered upon this subject for years.

The turmoil was catapulted by the 'Land Reform Programme' of the year 2000 which led to economic sanctions being imposed on Zimbabwe by global entities like the EU. The land reform program was preceded by large sums of money paid out to war veterans in the year 1997 as compensation for their participation in the liberation war which culminated in Zimbabwe's independence from British rule in 1980. Zimbabwe also supported the Zaire war and sent thousands of troops who were paid large sums of money after the war. This was the beginning of the end to a stable economy in Zimbabwe. The country started experiencing rising costs of living and high inflation as the Government battled to keep things under control. This saw mass exodus of people to neighbouring countries and overseas as people sought better opportunities. Chen falls into this category. She was in an abusive marriage and UK came as an escape route. She has not looked back ever since. Life can sometimes be cruel and she has seen it all. The Labour Party was in power when she moved to the UK on a visitor's visa more than twenty years ago. She had no plans of returning to Zimbabwe. The Labour Party was described as very lenient with undocumented migrants and it allowed them to work but things changed when the Conservatives took over.

"It's Molly Murombe. Tasvika." The voice on the other side of the phone said. Chen was startled by the voice because it had totally escaped her mind that three of the carers she had recruited from Zimbabwe were arriving on that day.

Welcome to London

She still had a busy day ahead of her and could not afford to go to Heathrow Airport to pick them up. For Molly – The drama began...

"Oh Hi Molly were you supposed to be coming today? I am really sorry it escaped my mind. So where are you now?" Chen said trying to figure out what to do.

Chen lived more than two hours away from Heathrow Airport. She still had five more clients to go to and by the time she finishes it will be dark anyway. This was a disaster. M25 is well known for heavy traffic. The congestion is terrible especially during peak hours. It becomes worse if there are car accidents because traffic police block lanes and leave only one or two open. There are normally long queues that may stretch for as long as five miles. Chen thought about all that and saw it as an impossibility to go and pick them up. She thought about the other few carers she had but all of them were busy with their care calls and she could not afford cancelling any of their calls.

Chen said, "Can you find security or the Information desk after I text you the post code and full address on WhatsApp. Ask for directions to the train station and take a train which comes here.

I will pick you up from the train station."

Molly had her bags and her two children with their own luggage. She took a trolley to load their stuff. The trolley was carrying six pieces and it was very heavy but the excitement of arriving in London left Molly not worrying much about the heavy bags. Molly had separated with her husband and their relationship was beyond repair so when the opportunity came to relocate, she grabbed it with both hands. She did not even want to leave her children

Welcome to London

because like most mothers, they were all she lived for. The living arrangements were something she never thought about but she didn't care as long as she had relocated to London. "How bad can it be anyway?" She comforted herself. The oldest was five and the youngest was three. It was not easy to push the trolley and carry the three-year old one on her back. Luckily she got some help from the other two who were recruited by the same care agency.

They each pushed their trolleys through the passages. There were a lot of people going towards their direction and opposite. They were in a different world and everything looked classy. Security officers were patrolling in nice looking uniforms. There were lights everywhere accompanied by a sweet scent. Everything was in order and seemingly saying, 'Welcome to London.'

They paced up and down trying to locate the information desk but they could not find it. They felt like they were looking for a needle in a haystack. It was not easy to ask from other people because none of them was confident enough to do that. At last they saw a black security officer who they had the confidence to approach.

"Excuse me Sir! Where is the train station?" Molly asked.

"Go straight, turn right, straight again, then left and you'll see it on your right." He said with a straight face.

"Thank you." They all said in unison.

After the security officer left, they all stood there transfixed because none of them got the directions. They gazed at each other wondering what to do next. Time was moving and they wished for some much needed rest because of fatigue. All of them were positive that the journey would not be very long but when they finally got to the train

Welcome to London

station, they were shocked to learn that it will take them close to two hours to reach their final destination. It was a hive of activity at the train station. There was not only one but many trains coming and going. They moved very fast and they did not stop for a very long time. The doors opened and closed automatically before the trains shot off. Loads of people were coming in and out as quickly as they could. Watching all this was quite a spectacle for Molly and her children.

The gentleman manning the ticket office was not very friendly. He wanted to get rid of Molly and company as quickly as he could. His answers were only made up of single words with a straight face.

"We are going to this address." Molly said as she turned the screen of her phone to face him.

"Ok." He said without looking at the phone. "How much?" Molly asked with a quiver in her voice "Single or return?" He asked.

Molly was confused and looked towards her two colleagues for redemption but they also shrugged their shoulders because they had no clue what the gentleman was talking about. There used to be passenger trains in Zimbabwe but this was in the distant past. Very few people would have chosen to use them anyway because they are very slow. Molly had never had the exposure to using trains as a mode of transport so this was all new. There was one passenger train which was revived to ply the Harare-Dzivarasekwa route but it was short-lived. The railway lines have mainly been left for goods trains. Some parts of the railway lines have shrubs and bushes growing because of either not being in use for a long time or not being maintained. The National Railways company itself is no

Welcome to London

longer as popular as it used to be because of reduced service. They used to recruit students for apprenticeship programmes which they no longer do at a large scale.

Molly wondered how her relationship status had anything to do with buying a ticket so she said, "I am single but I've got kids."

"I was referring to the ticket madam. Is it for a single journey or you will be returning?" He clarified with the longest sentence he had said since Molly and her colleagues got there.

"Oh! So sorry about the misunderstanding. Single. We are five." Molly felt very embarrassed. She wished she had asked for clarification before responding but it was now just water under the bridge.

"£65. Are you paying by card or cash?"

"Cash." Molly said as she reached for her wallet to pull out a few £20 sleeves which she counted to him. He quietly handed Molly five tickets and she stretched her hand to receive them.

"So which train are we getting?" Molly gathered the courage to ask.

"Next one coming." He said.

They thanked him and waited for what they thought was the last part of their journey. He was not interested in explaining much and Molly gathered confidence in that they were three adults so they were going to figure things out together. They shoved themselves into the next train with their big bags and everyone seemed to be looking at them wondering how they managed to carry so many bags. Instantly, the train took off. They found a few empty

Welcome to London

seats where they tucked themselves in anticipation of their journey.

By the time they disembarked from the train, It was very dark. The whole place was lit though and it was amazing how train stations were that busy. People seemed to use trains quite a lot. There were digital notice boards displaying arrival and departure times for trains going all over the places that Molly was not yet familiar with. On the floor, she saw a few men begging for some money.

"Can you spare some change please?" was their theme as each passenger passed in front of them. Some would give a few coins but some just ignored and proceeded with their journeys. There was another gentleman who was playing a guitar with his plate placed in front of him.

'First cut is the deepest! Baby I know! First cut is the deepest!' He played the popular song as he reminded Molly of her first love but it was not the time to think about that.

Molly reached for her phone but she did not have local network or data to make phone calls. She reached out to her colleagues and they were all in the same predicament. They approached someone and asked to make a phone call.

"It's Molly Murombe. Tasvika." She said with a deep sigh of relief

"Oh matosvika? I am still tied up at work for now manje moita sei?" Chen said as she tried to come up with a solution. She was quite aware that what she had done was not right but she did not have a choice.

"Ndiri kutozopedza almost midnight chaiyo." Chen said

Welcome to London

The 'manje moita sei' question baffled Molly because she had no idea where to go or where they were.

"If you ask at the train station where taxis are, they will show you. Get a taxi and go to the address I shared with you. If there are no taxis, call an uber."

"But we don't have phones to call. Tanga tatokumbirawo so that we can ask where to meet you." Molly said as things seemed to be getting muddled.

"Haa Molly! You want to tell me that three adults cannot make a plan to get a taxi? Ask the owner of the phone to call an uber for you. If he can't, Just ask the next person. I am busy with a client. Keep me in the loop." Chen said and dropped the call.

CHAPTER 6

Tee panicked out of a deep sleep. She opened her eyes and scanned through the room she was in. She was deeply shaken because it was an unfamiliar environment.

How did she even end up here?

She tried to lift her head but it was very heavy and she had a slight headache. Tee's heart started pounding as she tried to fill the memory gap that existed in her mind.

"What happened last night? Where am I?" She asked herself in a low voice trying to jog her memory.

On her left side, there was a stranger who was snoring and apparently in a deep sleep. "Who is this guy? Tee wondered! Is this Tim? Yes it's Tim." As she started to have a vague recollection of the events of the past twelve or so hours.

At the end of the bed she could see one leg of her Jean trousers hanging. She jumped out of bed but as soon as she did, she felt so much pain in her inner thighs. What she feared most might had happened. She was definitely naked and deflowered. There were slight blood stains on the bed sheets which covered the bed. She could see her pants lying on the floor and in panic she covered herself

Welcome to London

with a towel. Tee had lost her virginity! All of a sudden she felt deep anger steering inside her.

Did he rape her?

She asked the obvious question because evidence was all over the place. She started shedding tears of sorrow. It was never raining but pouring for her. From being kicked out to being raped. She had witnessed her world falling apart in less than a day.

Tee sat at the corner of the bed with her head in her hands. She felt very dirty and beat herself up for trusting a stranger. She started thinking about a lot of things as tears fell straight onto the carpet which sucked all of them gracefully . She felt robbed. She felt deceived. She felt let down. She felt humiliated.

"How could he?" The question went on and on in her head with no answer.

"So what's next for me? Tee asked herself in a low voice.

"What if I'm pregnant?" This question made her feel worse and she started crying the more.

This woke Tim up from his deep sleep and said with a sleepy voice,

"What's wrong babe. Why are you crying?"

"Are you serious asking me what is wrong?" Tee said amid sobs.

The anger inside Tee grew even more as Tim seemed relaxed about the whole situation. He actually stood up and pulled one cigarette from its pack and started smoking. He was not that bothered about the emotional Tee sitting at the edge of the bed. Tee looked through the

Welcome to London

flat for the first time. It was a studio flat so there was a small kitchen with a few plates in the sink. The toilet and shower were on the other side and from where she was sitting, Tee could see a bathing towel dangling. The studio flat was fairly clean. Tim had a double bed but the bed covers were not very clean. The room smelt of smoke because Tim had a habit of smoking indoors. Why would he care anyway because it appeared as if he lived alone. He had a television set and a small Radio on top of the washing machine.

"I don't really understand why you are upset. You were probably tired and I couldn't leave you at the Pub."

"That's not what I am talking about." She found it difficult to express herself because of not getting used to speaking in English all the time.

"You raped me!" Tee finally said it out

"Look at this!" She said pointing to the blood stains on the bed.

"Easy girl." Tim said looking at Tee with a sharp eye. "We both wanted it. You agreed to it so it wasn't rape. Maybe you are just regretting your decision but that does not make it rape. After all, you are in my house!"

Tee realised that this discussion was leading to a dead end. She just had to accept that she has faced a rocky start to life in London.

"Did you protect?" Tee asked with a sad voice. She had definitely no recollection of what happened and this all seemed like a dream to her.

"If this is a dream, why am I not waking up?" Tee asked herself

Welcome to London

Tim said, "I don't think so. I thought you were on some birth control method or something.

Most girls are." He said puffing on his cigarette as he pulled up his trousers.

"No I'm not Tim. Why should I be? I am not married!"

Tee said with so much resentment and anger. How could he assume such a thing. Tee later realised that Tim was correct that most girls take birth control measures even from an early age to avoid falling pregnant. Tee was being forced to adjust to the new way of life the hard way. She found herself exposed to a new culture she had never dreamt about. Girls can go to their General Practitioners and discuss birth control measures without their parents' consent. Tee did not see that happening where she came from.

"You have to go to the Pharmacy then." Tim said with little care.

Tim gave her a twenty pound note. Tee felt like a prostitute who was being paid for providing a service as she picked up the money. She did not have a choice because she was broke. Under normal circumstances, she would not have accepted the money from him. After refreshing, Tee packed her staff and headed to the Pharmacy but all she could think of along the way, was to end her miserable life. She had no money and now this? She was so hurt and broken inside. "What is the point of being alive?" Tee spoke to herself as she continued with a journey that started as a joke.

Time was not on her side. With no place to sleep, no money and no food, Tee saw no future in sight.

Welcome to London

Who can help in such a situation?

Tee dragged her bags as her mind roamed from point A to B. She was definite that there were a few other people walking along just like she was but she didn't take note of them.

"I think I should just kill myself."

It had never crossed her mind that at one point, she would have such dark thoughts. It sounded like a joke back home when stories of people committing suicide for one reason or the other circulated.

'Why would someone want to kill herself?' Tee used to wonder when she was growing up.

It is very easy to judge someone from the outside but at this point Tee was walking through a valley of utter darkness. Her mind and life were covered by thick darkness. She never stopped to check for cars as she crossed streets. She was sure that cars were hooting at her but her mind was very far. She was not blind but she could not see. She had been crying silently but fortunately her tears had dried up so no one took note of her pain. Her tears still flowed in her heart. A heart that had suffered deep stabs in the last day or two.

Right in front of her, a tall bridge appeared. The bridge had metal beams smiling in the light showers of rain which were also falling on Tee's dreams. The weather was not very nice for taking walks so Tee could only see a few, scattered people either dog-walking or seemingly distressed like her. She observed as one dog walker threw a ball in one direction while her dog chased after it with so much joy. The dog ran and leapt for the ball which it wrestled with for a few minutes before trotting back to its

Welcome to London

owner with the ball clutched between its teeth. Tee could not help but notice the joy in the dog's eyes. There was so much satisfaction projected from the dog's owner as they hugged and took off. It was paradoxical because Tee had no owner. Neither did she have anywhere to go. All she could live on were the joys of the distant past. Tee had not anticipated such a demise. With these thoughts, she was more convinced that being united with her maker was the only escape route. The tall bridge provided the perfect opportunity.

The silent river ran below the tall bridge. Water was flowing quietly just like the smooth rain. The architectural intelligence invested in the construction of the bridge impressed Tee because its legs were expertly designed. It reminded her of the famous Birchenough bridge in Zimbabwe which most older Zimbabweans know as a symbol on the old twenty cents coin. The bridge is built across the crocodile infested Save River. Each time Tee crossed it, she would say a little prayer because as a child, imaginations of the bridge collapsing while they were crossing were always dominant. Tee would imagine the crocodiles mobbing her dad's car and tearing them into pieces if the bridge collapses into the river. Back in the day, whenever Tee was sent to the shops by her dad, she got a reward of the twenty cents coin which she used to buy some popular sweets called 'sherbets.' She specifically liked them because they coloured her tongue in red which was enough evidence to show off to her friends.

As she slowly made her first steps across the bridge, she was counting down minutes. She scouted for a perfect spot to end it all. The miserable life has to come to an end – she convinced herself. The pain which she still felt from

Welcome to London

being raped, all of it wrapped around her heart! Right at the middle of the bridge, was the perfect spot because it led straight to the belly of the silent river. Tee had never learnt how to swim because she never had such an opportunity. She tried swimming several times when she visited her Grandparents during school holidays but she never managed the art. They used to go as a group to a nearby river but her trial only ended in the shallow waters where she with a few others kicked the water while holding tight to some grass on the river bank. It did not appear as if there were any Crocodiles to feast on her like in the Save river because she could see dogs swimming close to the river bank on the other side. It was now or never! Tee hoped that the silence in the river was what she was going to get when she meets her maker. She held that same belief like most people that when someone dies, they go straight to heaven even though there is no Biblical evidence for that. Whatever happened to her body – was not of substance at this moment. Tee dumped her belongings at the foot of the bridge and took off her heavy coat so that she could fit through the bars of the bridge. She took off her wet shoes and took hold of the metal bars. The only barrier between her and the river. The bridge was about twenty meters high and Tee hoped that the height would be enough to do the job. One leg was through and as she squeezed the second one, she heard a soft voice behind her saying,

"Hey dear! What's wrong? Would you mind talking about it?"

CHAPTER 7

Molly and her colleagues had a good view of the house the following day. They had just shoved themselves in when they arrived because it was rainy and cold so they did not have time to concentrate on details. It was a massive six bedroomed house which was built on two floors. From outside, the house did not look very big. It looked not so dilapidated but it could have done with a little touch-up outside. The inside of the house was nice and it was evident that the walls had been painted recently. They were allocated a room each and there were three other carers using bedrooms on the first floor so they had to settle for the top floor. They did not have much interaction with them because Molly and company arrived late and the other carers left early for their shift. Molly's children were living a dream as they enjoyed running up and down the stairs. They had never lived in a storey house before because most houses in Zimbabwe are bungalows. Storey houses are more common in low density areas but her children used to see them when they watched Nigerian movies. Molly was very tired but she heard the other carers leaving around 7am the following morning. Molly had not had a proper sleep since the night before her flight

Welcome to London

because of the hustles of packing and the anxiety of travelling.

She also recalled how hard she had hustled to raise about five thousand dollars required by the care agency to get sponsorship. On top of that, Molly required a few thousands for the tickets so by the time she left Zimbabwe, she was in about eight thousand dollars' worth of debt. "First month I would have returned all your monies. Don't worry." Said Molly as she reassured Grace who lent her part of the money.

"I hope so because that's all I have as capital for my business. Haundinyudzi iwe?" Grace said a bit worried.

"Why would I do that to my best friend? I can't bite the hand that fed me." Molly said as she continued to give promises to Grace.

"Iiii Molly, when you get there you will forget about us and disappear from the radar like the Titanic." Grace said accompanying her remarks with a giggle.

"Not at all Chommie. Why would I do that? You know me very well." Molly explained. "Who knows? Maybe you would have found a white man and married him." She said teasing Molly who went into fits of laughter.

"If you disappear, I will go to your rural home and sell your grandfather's cows to recover my money." Grace continued and they both laughed as the issue seemed to have been resolved.

Molly had never flown before and she tried to imagine the experience throughout the night. Her room had a double bed which she had to share with her two children and a small wardrobe in the corner. There was a small fridge

Welcome to London

which looked very new planted in the other corner. With those three items, the room was almost full. There was hardly any space left for Molly and her children's bags.

"How can a room be so small?" Molly wondered as she scanned through the tiny room to find space for their luggage.

She later learnt that the kitchen was two floors down which was accessible to everyone. Molly tried to acquaint herself with the new environment by remembering the short conversation she had with the other carers who jogged them through basic house rules.

"This is the kitchen." One carer called Mercy said. "It is accessible to everyone but you can keep your food in your rooms."

"There are two bathrooms, one on the first floor and the other one on the second floor." Mercy continued. "There are two toilets next to the bathrooms so we are all going to share." She said pointing to upstairs.

The excitement soon faded into sorrow for Molly and her little ones as reality started sinking in. The challenges of adjusting to a new environment started taking a toll on them. The experience was different for Molly, her children and her colleagues. Each had their own fair share of problems to mourn about. The famous Shona Proverb says, 'Kusina amai hakuendwe' loosely translated to mean that one should not stray far from their mother's umbilical cord. The children were worried about spending most of their time cooked up inside. They were used to spending much of their time running around and playing with friends. None of that could happen because once or twice, Molly had received a few complaints from next door

Welcome to London

neighbours about her kids making noise. The contrast between previous and current life was as visible as daylight.

Back home, the day would start by going out and meeting a few friends to play football in the streets. The teams gradually expanded as the morning progressed because of waking up at different times. The art of making plastic footballs had been mastered by Molly's son. Girls did not want to be left out so they made their own net balls. Girls normally spent time playing with their dolls, playing pada and netball. There were no designated playing areas in the ghetto so kids tend to just make up their own playing areas. The freedom for Molly's kids to just go out to play without adult supervision soon vanished like mist as they were being introduced to the new way of life. The parks were nice but the weather was not always pleasant. Much of the time it would be rainy, cloudy and freezing which limited their exposure to the outside world.

Molly started learning about 'Safeguarding' and 'negligence' which meant that she could not let her children out without adult supervision. As a single mother, Molly wondered how things would work out for her. It was also astonishing to learn that younger children are dropped off and picked up from school. Most schools do not offer transport and it is the responsibility of the parent to manage school run. Her headache started when she thought about managing work and school run. Molly was employed as a domiciliary care worker and working less hours translated to less money which leads to financial challenges. The bills also required attention as she was supposed to pay for gas, electricity, broadband and rent. The total amount for bills would leave Molly struggling to

Welcome to London

make ends meet. Her stress level shot up because she was not made aware of all that before relocating. Some carers had to work night shifts so that they could do school run but the agency Molly worked for did not have any night shifts to offer. The second challenge she faced was that children could not be left alone at home after they return from school. They need someone to babysit them. Molly's situation seemed more complex than the poverty she was running away from. With eyes around her, Molly could not afford to put a foot wrong. When they started at full swing, she did not even have the privilege of seeing her colleagues. Molly relied on work mates to manage school run which she had to pay for. All her house mates were either single or they had left their children in Zimbabwe.

Molly had never been exposed to such a job as she started adjusting to the new role. Time always seemed to be of paramount importance as her day started very early and ended very late. The first month was a steep learning curve mainly because Molly did not drive. She was normally paired with someone who had a car and if she wasn't she had to rely on public transport. The horrible weather made life very difficult for her because some of the clients were located far from bus stops. The expenses of paying for transport to and from work started taking a toll on her because she had not yet been paid her first salary. The agency had provided a meagre five hundred pounds for sustenance but it quickly disappeared with daily expenses. Molly had to make arrangements with house mates who would not be on shift to manage school run and look after the children. That was an extra expense as she had to fork out money to pay baby sitters. Life became very complex before she even appreciated being in the UK.

Welcome to London

By the end of the first month, Molly felt drained and ill but she had no option but to go on. After a few weeks, her feet were swollen because of too much walking and she had very little time to eat. Molly had already lost a few kilograms and things started taking a toll on her. Her day started around 7am and until after 10pm. She had very little interaction with other carers who she shared the house with because of conflicting rotas. Molly was not only struggling with work related issues but when the salary came in, she almost collapsed because it was just a meagre amount. She just could not afford to settle her debt in Zimbabwe and meet all the bills. It was on a Friday evening when it so happened that Molly and her two colleagues finished work early and got home around 9pm. They were all in the kitchen cooking the traditional Sadza dish. They had decided to share the meal. In the kitchen, the silence was unusual. Molly was in a low mood because her salary was not even enough to cover her bills and daily expenses. She decided to break the silence and said,

"Did you check your account?"

There was a long pause before her colleagues said, "Yes I did." In unison. There was another long pause before Molly coughed and shifted her chair towards the heater to catch more heat. "I don't understand how it was calculated." One colleague said as he shook his head in disbelief.

"Me neither." Another colleague said,

"I thought I worked more hours than that. I don't even get how some of the deductions were calculated."

There was another long pause as they digested their sorrows. The sombre atmosphere was synonymous to a funeral wake. Molly's children who usually made noise

Welcome to London

were already in bed ready for another long day ahead of them. They had their own worries but not enough to stop them from snoring until day break.

"Haa Hapana zvatiri kuita guys. We are doing nothing." Molly said as she sighed deeply. "I don't even understand how my mileage was calculated." Another colleague said as she introduced her own worry.

She had a little money saved up so when she arrived, she was helped by some workmates to get a small car to use for work which made her life easy but she was supposed to be paid mileage since she was using her personal car for work purposes.

Having time off work was not guaranteed and they never had fixed days which made it very difficult to do any meaningful planning. At times, Molly would work for seven consecutive days without a break. People complained but those who petitioned the owner had their hours reduced significantly and they started struggling to make ends meet. Most carers had to desist from complaining because of fear of having their working hours reduced. Work and life balance was just not visible especially for those single. Most people just spent their time sleeping because of the much needed rest. Those who drive felt more pain because of doing a double job. All the imaginations of travelling across UK to see places quickly went through the window because money is just not enough to do that and time is a scarce commodity. The fantasies of seeing lovely men and women for dating never comes to fruition as they realise that UK is a work driven economy with very little opportunities for social life. Most carers fall into working class and life is mostly about living from hand to mouth. Besides their own immediate responsibilities in the

Welcome to London

UK, most immigrants have to support their siblings and extended family back home. Societal pressure means that they also have to invest back home so that they have tangible items as evidence of their time abroad.

Not only did Molly struggle with financial issues but her mental health started to spiral out of control. Molly was living in a house full of people but she was lonely. She was bombarded by constant call from people she owed which caused her significant levels of stress. She was just not working enough to manage all her expenses and the guilt of betraying people who trusted her took a toll on her. There was no one to talk to because all the people around her, had their own issues to worry about. However, Molly had to continue soldiering on for the sake of her little ones. She put a brave face and smile like what most mothers do even though her own health was falling apart like a damp slice of bread. Molly struggled with sleep and she would spend most nights wondering when things were going to get better.

It so happened that on her day off, Molly decided to go for a walk before picking up her kids from school. The weather was not very pleasant but she needed to clear her mind. She put on her shoes and grabbed her coat which weighed a few kilograms. There was a lovely bridge where seeing water flowing silently soothed her and gave her comfort. Molly had seen a lot of people standing and looking into the river as if it provided some answers to secret puzzles. She decided to try it and since then, it turned into a therapeutic habit for her. She had not met many black people at the bridge. Most people were white who normally took their dogs for walks along the river. She had met a few very lovely white people who always smiled and

Welcome to London

waved at her. She usually returned the favour and proceeded with her journey. She took a few coins with her to buy some sweets for her children - The few of the remaining. She was left with less than ten pounds in her wallet but payday was not yet in sight. She breathed deeply and just said, "**Welcome to London**."

Silent showers greeted Molly as she stepped out of the door. The cloudy sky was something usual because ever since she moved to the UK, she had not seen much sun. She was starting to learn about the seasons mainly from her children who were taught at school. She started to understand why dark people become light skinned in the UK because their skin is not always exposed to heat for the most part of the year. With those thoughts, she started off towards the bridge to offload her sorrows.

CHAPTER 8

Molly approached the bridge as usual but as she lifted her eyes, she was shocked to see someone trying to squeeze through the iron bars. She adjusted her eyes to catch a better view but she could not believe her eyes. Molly scanned around like a vulture looking for some prey but she realised that there was no one else around. The only few people in sight were enjoying the silent showers while playing with their dogs. She wiped dribbling water off her brows and her eyes were definitely not deceiving her.

'What is happening?'

Molly quizzed herself as she quickened her pace towards the lofty bridge. For a moment, she forgot about her children and her personal worries to get to the bottom of what was taking place. Time was not on her side because it was almost 3pm and soon, her children would be peeping through the classroom window to see whether she had arrived or not. Pupils are not let out of their classrooms until a parent or guardian arrives to pick them up. Failure to be on time has its own consequences on parents. Molly was normally on time because she did not want any concerns raised about her parenthood. As most mothers do, she tried to conceal her own pain so that her

Welcome to London

children can be happy. She did not want to be viewed as struggling to look after them as a single parent. What also put pressure on Molly was that she tried to compensate for her children's absent father and this caused her so much stress and strain. She felt bad for her children. The decision to relocate was in her children's best interest because she wanted to provide a better life for them. Her children had asked some tough questions about their father and it haunted her not to be with their father but there was nothing she could do. Molly noticed that as they grew, their curiosity also grew and they start asking questions.

"Why did you leave dad back home?" They asked her as they were preparing to have dinner. Molly took a very long pause before responding because she knew she had to be very careful with her words.

"Vachatevera zvavo at some point." She said trying to be as general as possible so that the case is laid to bed but her assumption was wrong.

"Why is it when we were still in Zimbabwe, dad lived somewhere else? John's dad and mum lived together."

Her son asked with curiosity on his face. He definitely intended to solve a puzzle that appeared to have boggled his mind for a long time. This is the kind of discussion Molly was not prepared for after a long day at work but she knew she had to be very calm to avoid snapping at them.

She thought of diverting their attention to something else by saying,

"Can you go and call auntie Tee for dinner please?"

They both trotted to the bedroom where they all shared the tiny room with their new visitor, auntie Tee. Ever since

Welcome to London

she started living with them a few weeks ago, she had been helping Molly with school run as she sorted her own stuff after the incident at the bridge. Tee was a joy around the children and they liked her so much. This was partly to do with spending a lot of time with them after school and going for walks. Tee had not been herself for a few weeks and as such needed rest slowly brought her back on track. Molly's experience with kids and maturity helped her to support Tee to get back on her feet. Tee suffered flashbacks and she exhibited signs of trauma including panic attacks and hallucinations. Molly did not want to put any pressure on her so that she fully recuperated. Molly and Tee were not related but they started supporting each other as if they were blood sisters. Tee had introduced Molly to her parents after the incident and they had created a bond. Such is life in a foreign land. Family is not always about blood but positive relationships. Most people who share the same totem have managed to create long lasting bonds even though they had been total strangers.

"So why did we not live with dad?"

Her son asked as he dug into his plate of Sadza.

They all sat at the table and her son was still expecting a legitimate response. Apparently, the diversion tactic had not worked for Molly so she had to find another way of addressing the issue. She pondered for a while as she tried to find proper words but nothing was forthcoming. Her son was maturing faster than she expected. She felt so much pressure but as the adult, she calmed herself down and said,

"He did not like staying in Mabvuku." Is the answer that randomly sprang to her mind but she was not even convinced by her own answer.

Welcome to London

"So he didn't like us?" Her daughter questioned with so much disappointment in her face

Molly realised that the issue was getting out of hand. She had differences with their dad but she had no intention of creating a wedge between the children and their father. If anything, she made an effort for him to be as involved as possible.

"No my darling. Not you but the place." Molly said hoping that the answer would satisfy them. "But then why did we not go to live with him where he lived?" Another legit question sprang up to Molly's disappointment.

"Ok enough about your dad. Let's prepare for bed now because tomorrow you have school!" Tee said with a beaming smile. She bailed Molly out because she realised how she was becoming more and more uncomfortable with the discussion.

Molly's thoughts raced to and fro as she made strides towards the bridge trying to remember how to react to such a critical situation. Her mind was hauled back from wander land as she tried to think about a solution. It happens most of the time that impromptu situations can only be reflected upon moments after the situation resolves.

"First rule – Don't panic. Second rule – Call 999. Third rule – Try to talk to the victim…". Molly recited as she got closer. Her fingers were running through the phone's keypads as she dialled 999. It did not take long for the call to be answered and She started having a conversation with someone on the other end of the phone. Molly lowered her voice as she passed on the details requested by the operator:

Welcome to London

"We are at the bridge."

"Female. No one else is around."

"No blood that I can see."

Molly went on as she approached the scene. She was told that emergency services were on their way. As she got closer, she started to have a better view and she could see that the victim was a black, young lady who appeared to be in so much distress.

Molly almost ran out of words and she took a deep breath. It was a critical moment because the young lady was ready to take a leap. Molly did not want to shout, so she calmed herself down and in a soft and audible voice, she said,

"Hey dear! What's wrong? Would you mind talking about it?" Molly said as she was not sure if she had used the right words to deescalate the situation.

"I just want to die. Ndiregei ndife!"

Molly's heart skipped because she recognised the accent and the language. The young lady went into a fit of sobs. Molly reached out her hand and started praying in her heart.

"**Welcome to London**" Molly sighed as she tried to come to terms with what was in front of her.

"That was a close shave." She said as soon as the young lady came to safety.

YouTube, Facebook, Instagram, Tiktok, Threads & X

@ Elliot Msindo The Poet elliotmsindo@gmail.com

Printed in Great Britain
by Amazon